WI

TWO SHORT STORIES IN ONE VOLUME

Charlie Megahey

ARTHUR H. STOCKWELL LTD
Torrs Park, Ilfracombe, Devon, EX34 8BA
Established 1898
www.ahstockwell.co.uk

First published in Great Britain, 2016

British Library Cataloguing-in-Publication Data.
A catalogue record for this book is available
from the British Library.

ISBN 978-0-7223-4660-0
Printed in Great Britain by
Arthur H. Stockwell Ltd
Torrs Park Ilfracombe
Devon EX34 8BA

BOOK ONE

"WHO'S A LOSER NOW, THEN?"

CONTENTS

INTRODUCTION

Britain was at war with Germany; many cities and towns had been bombed by the German Air Force.

The British government had decided to evacuate the children to the safety of the countryside.

CHAPTER ONE

LEAVING HOME

Emma and her mother stood on the platform at Southampton Railway Station watching the train come streaming in. The huffing and puffing of the train as it entered the station made Emma more nervous than she had felt before; she was feeling worried and unhappy about leaving home.

"You will come for me if I don't like the school, won't you, Mum?"

"Of course I will, love, but just give yourself a chance to get used to it, won't you?" her mother answered, wiping a tear from her eye, wondering if she had made the right decision in agreeing to Emma being evacuated.

Of course it was the right thing to do, she thought. What with the bombs coming down, Emma's father away in the army and she herself working in the aircraft factory down by Southampton Docks, Emma would be far safer away in the countryside.

"Go on, get on the train before I change my mind," her mother said, helping her onto the train with her suitcase and seeing her settled into a carriage already occupied by three other girls.

Emma later found out that the girls were from

Portsmouth and were going to the same school as she was.

Emma sat quietly looking out the open window, trying to keep a stiff upper lip as the train roared into life. She watched the figure of her mother slowly fading out of sight before her very eyes.

CHAPTER TWO

OAKTREE MANOR

"Salisbury Station – next stop Salisbury Station" came the announcement.

Emma and the girls were met in the car park by an elderly bearded man who introduced himself as Fred the school gardener. He then escorted them to a small bus parked in a side street near the railway station.

Once seated on the bus, Fred turned to the girls with a large smile on his face and declared, "It won't take long, about half an hour at the most if the road is clear. Sit back and relax yourselves."

The journey was conducted in silence and after what seemed like ages the bus turned sharply into a narrow country lane before stopping on the forecourt of a large Georgian house situated in two acres of serene Wiltshire countryside. The house had seen better days; the building was surrounded with scaffolding planks, concrete mixers, numerous bricks and ladders. Despite this Emma thought it was the most beautiful house she had ever seen in her life.

Emma and the girls followed Fred up the steps to the front door as he explained that the house had previously been a smart stately home of a wealthy businessman and had also been used as a hospital for wounded soldiers during the First World War. The elegant rooms were now converted into dormitories and classrooms for fifty pupils and residential accommodation for the school staff.

The door was opened by a tall, thin girl dressed in a dark pleated skirt and a white blouse; she also wore a red armband around her forearm.

"Come in and follow me," she ordered.

Emma and the girls followed in silence as they were led along the narrow corridor to a room with a 'Headmistress' sign above the door. They were ushered into the room where a long wooden bench was placed in front of a desk.

"Sit down. Miss Bellows will see you in a minute," the girl said, closing the door as she left the room.

Emma and the girls sat uneasily taking in their new environment. There was a large bookcase crammed full of books, a map of the world on one wall and a picture of the royal family on another.

The door opened and in walked a small, stocky woman dressed in a dark-brown full-length uniform. Hanging from her belt was a large bunch of keys that rattled with every step she took.

"Stand up when I enter the room," she barked.

The girls jumped to their feet in unison. Emma was shaking so much she thought her legs would give way and she would collapse to the floor. She steadied herself, took a deep breath and stared straight ahead.

The keys jangled on the woman's hips as she walked across the room. Then she sat herself down and shuffled some papers on the large desk in front of her.

"Sit," she commanded.

The girls sat down in unison.

"I am Miss Bellows. I am the head teacher here at Oaktree Manor and you will address me as Miss Bellows at all times. I make the rules here and what I say goes. Do you understand?" she hissed through clenched teeth.

"Yes, Miss Bellows," the girls answered nervously.

"Right then, let's see who we have here. Jane Richards?"

One of the girls Emma had been sat with in the train carriage put her hand up as she looked down at her feet.

"Don't be so impertinent, girl," shouted Miss Bellows. "Look at me when I am talking and answer me. Do you understand?"

"Yes, Miss Bellows."

"Good. Let's start again, then, shall we?"

Miss Bellows called out the names of the girls one by one.

"Jane Richards?"

"Yes, Miss Bellows."

"Catherine Brown?"

"Yes, Miss Bellows."

"Emma Baker?"

"Yes, Miss Bellows."

"Rose Davidson?"

"Yes, Miss Bellows."

Miss Bellows sniffed loudly, then rose from her seat and strode across the room. "I suppose you're missing your mammies?" she taunted with a tight grin on her face as she spoke. "Well, I'm the mammy here and I won't take any nonsense at my school. Do you understand me?"

"Yes, Miss Bellows."

"Any girl breaking the rules will be severely dealt with by me. Do you understand me?"

"Yes, Miss Bellows," came the now rehearsed reply.

"Good – I'm glad we understand one another," she said, reaching to the side of her desk to press a button.

With that the door opened and in walked the tall, thin girl who had showed the girls in when they arrived.

"Nelly, take these girls to get their uniform; show them to the wash area and see that they get their evening meal."

"Yes, Miss Bellows," came Nelly's reply, and she promptly guided the girls out of the room.

As they walked around the school with Nelly, Emma wondered what the rules were. Miss Bellows hadn't actually said, but no doubt there would be many and the punishments would be severe if they were broken.

The dining room was very noisy with chit-chat and laughter. The girls were shown by Nelly where to get their food and where to sit. The food served was sparse and it consisted of weak tea, and a slice of bread and butter followed by a small bowl of tapioca pudding.

Emma, Jane, Catherine and Rose were all sat together and the conversation between them was friendly; they all got on well. They were starting to relax a little in their new surroundings when suddenly a girl on the table behind theirs turned around and with one hand pulled Emma's hair and with her other hand stole the bread from Emma's plate. Emma protested and tried to retrieve her food, when she noticed the girl who had stolen her food was Nelly.

"Come on, then," Nelly said, "let's see how brave you are?" Nelly's face was contorted and menacing.

Emma decided that it wasn't worth fighting for and turned back to her new friends.

Nelly started laughing and started a chorus of chants with, "Loser, loser, who's a loser?"

The dining hall was silent for a moment and then the rest of the girls in the hall all joined in with Nelly: "Loser, loser, who's a loser?"

Jane, Catherine and Rose just looked on, speechless. They didn't know what to do.

But then just as quickly as it started there was silence in the room again. The chit-chat and laughter started up again and it was as if nothing at all had happened as things got back to normal.

CHAPTER THREE

THE PUNISHMENT

The girls in the dormitory awoke to the loud rattle of keys being rolled across the iron bedsteads.

"Out girl, out girl." The order came to the rattle of keys.

The girls scrambled out of bed and lined up at the bottom of their bunks. Miss Bellows paced up and down in front of them, staring menacingly into each girl's face.

"One or more of you has been up to mischief and I intend to find out who it was," she said with a smirk on her face. "I want to know who the culprits are – who has been defacing the noticeboard on the wall outside dormitory three."

The girls stood still; not a sound could be heard except for the sound of the rattling keys as Miss Bellows continued to pace up and down the aisle.

"Right then, you lot, I'll show you who the boss here is. Did I not warn you that if anyone broke the rules they would be severely dealt with? As no one has owned up you will all be punished," she said, ordering the girls out of the dormitory still in their nightclothes.

As they walked along the corridor Emma noticed the writing in chalk on the noticeboard. 'Skinny Nelly

– Rubber Belly', it read.

Emma stifled a giggle as it dawned on her that this was probably the reason they were being punished. She had no idea who had written it, but she felt a sense of justice that Nelly deserved it.

Miss Bellows marched the girls out into the snow-covered yard, where it was so cold it took their breath away. The girls were ordered to form a straight line as Miss Bellows continued to walk up and down.

"I am going to give one last chance for the person responsible to own up or the lot of you could be out here all night," she hissed, with a slight grin on her face.

The girls remained silent.

"Have it your way, then," barked Miss Bellows, and with a huff turned and walked back into the school leaving the girls outside wearing nothing but their nightclothes in the freezing snow.

"I bet that stupid Nelly wrote it herself," Jane said through frozen teeth.

"She probably did it just to get us in trouble," replied Rose.

"I'm sorry, girls – I know we didn't do it, but maybe it's because Nelly didn't like me. That's why she is causing trouble for us," Emma said, feeling that she was to blame.

Jane, Rose and Catherine all answered together, "It's not your fault, Emma. It could have been any one of us sat behind her in the dining hall, and she could have picked on any of us."

It was then Emma felt a new strength she didn't know she had.

"Thank you," she replied shyly, wiping a tear from her eye.

The girls could feel the cold, biting snow going through their bodies; the flimsy nightclothes gave no protection whatsoever. They shuffled around and clasped hands, trying to install some warmth.

Although it seemed like for ever, it was twenty minutes later that the school door opened and Miss Bellows came strolling out into the yard.

"Right then," she barked, "I think you've learnt the lesson, you do not deface school property. About turn," she ordered.

With that the girls were marched back into the school along the corridor and back to the welcome warmth of their beds.

CHAPTER FOUR

THE FIGHT

The day started bright and sunny. Emma felt good – she had enjoyed her breakfast of dried egg on toast. The dried egg that came in cartons was not to everyone's liking, but Emma loved it.

It was the weekend, and she and her new friends, Jane, Rose and Catherine, were enjoying a game of hopscotch when suddenly Emma lunged forward from a punch in the back. Turning round, she could see Nelly standing over her laughing and singing: "Loser, loser, loser."

Emma could stand it no longer and with a mighty shove she sent Nelly reeling backwards. Within seconds they were rolling on the ground, scratching and pulling each other's hair.

All the other girls stood around the fighting girls chanting, "Emma, Emma, Emma. We want Emma."

Suddenly a booming voice could be heard: "What's going on here?"

It was Miss Bellows and in a swift action she grabbed both girls by the scruff of their necks, pulling them up to their feet.

"It was her, Miss; she attacked me for no reason,

Miss," sighed Nelly with a fake sob as she rubbed her eyes with a handkerchief.

Emma tried to protest, but it was to no avail.

Miss Bellows shouted, "Quiet – I've heard enough." Then she instructed one of the girls watching to fetch her cane from the office.

Emma stood still, knowing that she was going to get punished even though she hadn't started the fight.

The girl returned with the cane and, without warning, Miss Bellows flexed it and brought it down with an almighty ‘whack, whack, whack’.

Emma tried her best to be brave; she held herself back from screaming despite the pain being so excruciating. She didn’t want Nelly to get the satisfaction of seeing her cry.

“Please, Miss Bellows; please, Miss Bellows, it wasn’t me. I didn’t start it,” Emma pleaded, but again her words went unheard and she felt the stinging ‘whack, whack, whack’ of the cane as it landed on her posterior.

“That will teach you not to start brawling in the schoolyard. Take this as a warning – it will be more severe next time. Now go and clean yourself up and then clean the toilets and washroom as an additional punishment,” Miss Bellows ordered with a dismissive gesture.

As Emma turned to walk away she could see Nelly standing with a large grin on her face and gesturing with her lips: “Loser, loser, loser.”

CHAPTER FIVE

SPORTS DAY

It was sports day, and loud music blared from the Tannoy in between the announcements.

"Run, rabbit, run, rabbit, run, run, run. Don't let the farmer get his gun, gun, gun. . . ."

Emma was entered into the one-mile race; she had got through all the heats easily and now it was time for the final race. There were seven other girls in the final and they were lined up ready and waiting to go. Nelly was one of the eight girls in the race and had positioned herself slightly behind Emma in the second row.

"Are you ready? On your marks. Get set. Go."

'Bang!' They were off. Emma felt the tug on her vest as Nelly went past, and soon she and the other girls were yards in front, but Emma didn't let it bother her. She knew they had gone off too fast. Slowly but surely she caught up and overtook the other girls one by one. Emma was going faster and faster until there was only big Nelly left to overtake.

Nelly was slowing down. She was beginning to tire. Puffing and blowing, she knew she was beaten. Emma was now alongside her and, with a brief turn of her head and a beaming smile on her face, she declared,

"See yer – wouldn't wanna be yer."

She broke through the finishing tape to the loud cheers from the watching crowd.

As all the girls crowded around her, Emma felt elated. It was the best moment of her life: she had beaten Nelly in front of the whole school and it felt great.

She was taken aback when Miss Bellows tapped her on her back and said, "Well done. Congratulations."

CHAPTER SIX

GOING HOME

With her suitcase packed and her gas mask slung loosely over her shoulder, Emma sat quietly outside Miss Bellows' office. At last the hoped- and prayed-for letter had arrived and she was going home. The letter was from her mum, telling her that her father was home from the war, and that she and her father would be coming down to collect her and take her back home.

Emma was delighted – at last she was going home. Her thoughts turned to the day she had arrived and how nervous she was. But now she was going home, having conquered her fears. She was going home a winner.

The front door opened – it was Nelly accompanied by Emma's parents. Emma jumped up from her seat and ran over and hugged her mum and dad, who couldn't contain their happiness at seeing their daughter after all the months she had been away.

Emma's mother bent down to pick up her suitcase; but she was interrupted by Nelly, who grabbed hold of the suitcase and gruffly said, "That's my job. I'll do that."

Emma could see that Nelly was annoyed that she

was going home and that she had been summoned by Miss Bellows to escort her parents and carry her suitcase out to the car for her. Nelly kept her head bowed and shuffled along, not taking her eyes from the ground.

When they reached the car park Emma reached out to shake hands. She thanked Nelly, but couldn't help feeling a sense of achievement, and with a twitch of a smile a thought passed through her mind but never left her lips. What she was really wanting to say was:

"Who's a loser now, then?"

BOOK TWO

“NOW YOU’VE GOT TO BELIEVE US: WE’RE THE TEAM THAT WON THE CUP”

CONTENTS

OAKWOOD

CHAPTER ONE

OAKWOOD

The boys from Oakwood Secondary School were jumping with joy, as their football team had just qualified for the final of the County Youth Cup against their old rivals, St George's College. St George's College had won the cup twice before, but this was the first time Oakwood had managed to reach the final.

Oakwood Secondary School was situated within the Southend district of Oakwood. This was the oldest part of the town, with its two-up-and-two-down terraced dwellings. None of the houses had gardens, just tiny backyards to the rear. Some still had their old outside toilets, which were built shortly after the First World War.

Five minutes' walk up the High Street, through the park and past the St George's College playing fields you came into the more affluent district of Oakwood, with its leafy streets, detached houses and large gardens back and front.

CHAPTER TWO

THE PAPER ROUND

"Jon-Joe, Jon-Joe, get out of bed. You're late for your paper round. And don't forget you've got football practice this afternoon," Jon-Joe's mother called out to him before leaving to go to work at the local hospital, where she was employed as a cleaner on the wards.

Jon-Joe jumped out of bed and, with a quick splash of water on his face, he was straight into his football shirt and trainers before bolting down the stairs to devour the milk and sandwiches his mother had left for him on the kitchen table.

Jon-Joe and his mother were inseparable since his father had passed away of cancer at an early age. Life was hard for both of them, but his mother would just take things in her stride.

"Don't worry," she would say, "we'll get by. There's a lot of people worse off than we are," she would say with a loving hug and kiss.

"I know you are right, Mum, but things will get better for us when I become a professional footballer," Jon-Joe would answer with the confidence of his youth.

Jon-Joe really enjoyed doing his paper round. The

customers were nice, and the tips came in handy for buying his football kit, but he was always wary when approaching 33 Acacia Road – 33 Acacia Road was where Big Manny lived.

Big Manny, was a student at St George's College. He was also the central defender of their football team – Oakwood's opponents in the County Youth Cup final. Big Manny was also known in Oakwood as the town bully, who took great enjoyment in picking on boys who were much smaller than himself.

Jon-Joe always did his best to keep out of Manny's way. But sooner or later he would bump into him and have to suffer the nasty name-calling followed by the odd dig in the ribs.

Jon-Joe approached No. 33 with caution. He could hear boys talking, and there was a potent smell of stale tobacco coming from a large tent that had been pitched in the centre of the front garden. Jon-Joe delivered the paper to No. 33 as quietly as he could, but on turning around there was Manny with three smaller boys; they were blocking his path as he tried to make his way out to the gate.

"So we meet again, squirt." Manny sniggered, moving his face closer to Jon-Joe's.

Jon-Joe tried his best to move away. He could smell the stale tobacco on Manny's breath.

Manny reached out and took a firm grip of the collar of Jon-Joe's football shirt. "Where did you get this? Did your mammy buy it in a second-hand shop?" he asked with a menacing look on his face.

"Go on, Manny. You tell him what's what. We can't have these Southend scruffs coming into our district as if they own it," quipped one of the smaller boys.

Manny tightened his grip on Jon-Joe's shirt and pulled him closer. Jon-Joe tried to pull away, but to no avail.

"What's going on here, then?" a loud voice at the gate asked. It was the postman doing his rounds.

Manny hesitated as the tall postman approached.

"We – we were only playing, mister." Manny stuttered his words.

"Doesn't look like playing to me," the postman stated.

Manny reluctantly loosened his grip on Jon-Joe's shirt as the postman moved closer.

"Leave the boy alone. I've been watching you for some time now and I'm sure your parents wouldn't want to know about you bullying boys smaller than yourself," the postman said as he positioned himself between the two boys, enabling Jon-Joe to break free.

"Thanks, mister," Jon-Joe shouted with delight as he bolted out the gate and up the hill to the playing fields as fast as his legs would carry him.

CHAPTER THREE

FOOTBALL PRACTICE

The football practice was going well – Jon-Joe did not let the earlier encounter with Big Manny affect his play.

He loved his football – football was his life. He knew he was good; many people had told him that he was good. He was quick and with his amazing trickery and ball skills many people had started to take notice of him. A report in the evening paper after the County Youth Cup semi-final stated, 'The boy playing on the left wing for Oakwood was good. I'm sure that the football scouts will be keeping an eye on this young lad. He's one of the best young prospects I've seen for a very long time.'

"That's it, lads. Practice is over for the day," the coach said as he gathered his team around in a circle. "Now for the big one. Let's go and show them college boys what we are made of."

Then with a great flood of enthusiasm Jon-Joe and his teammates joined hands chanting:

"Oakwood, Oakwood, Oakwood,
Yay! Yay! Yay!
Oakwood, Oakwood, Oakwood,
Yay! Yay! Yay!"

CHAPTER FOUR

THE FINAL

The big day had arrived – it was the final of the County Youth Cup.

"It's the final curtain."

The music from the Tannoy blared out around the ground as the teams kicked off. Both teams were well matched in the early stages, but it wasn't long before St George's College scored against the run of play.

Oakwood probed for an equaliser, but to no avail. They were getting nowhere fast, when the coach decided to change the style of play.

"Jon-Joe, over here," he called out from the dugout. "I want you to change to the right wing. That's their weakest point. If we are going to win this game it will be from that side," he shouted, cheering the boys on.

Jon-Joe was enjoying the game more now. The changes had made the difference – he was receiving the ball more often and had much more space. His legs just seemed to flow over the ground and with great acceleration he went by one defender after another until he reached Big Manny. Taking him onto the right, then he dummied to the left before letting go with a thunderball shot straight over the goalkeeper's head and into the left-hand side of the net.

Jon-Joe ran in to retrieve the ball. He could see Manny was furious.

"Just you wait – I'll get you next time, you little squirt," Manny snarled through his clenched teeth.

Jon-Joe took no notice.

The game had sprung to life. The Oakwood supporters were waving their scarfs while dancing and singing: "Oakwood, Oakwood, Oakwood – we love Oakwood."

With time running out and the score 1–1 with three minutes extra being declared, Jon-Joe received the ball from a throw-in. He glided up the pitch and into the opponents' box until he reached Big Manny, but this time Big Manny was ready for him. He didn't even try to play the ball. He just poleaxed him straight to the ground a foot from the penalty spot. The referee ran over; showing his annoyance, he blew his whistle, reached into his pocket, pulled out the red card and sent Manny off.

Jon-Joe got up and dusted himself down. He wasn't going to let anyone else take the penalty kick. Knowing time was short, he placed the ball on the spot then took a short run-up and BANG, the ball was in the net. Game over! Oakwood had won the cup 2–1.

Jon-Joe was delighted – it was the best moment of his life, and everyone crowded around and patted him on the back, congratulating him. The supporters lifted him onto their shoulders and carried him around the pitch, singing:

"Now you've got to believe us:
We're the team that won the cup.
Now you've got to believe us:
We're the team that won the cup."